The Game that never was

Ope Afeni

First Published by Bounty Press Ltd

New Edition

ISBN - 978-978-785-999-5

Published by:

Opem Publishing Ltd
2nd Floor, Suite 41,
Crosstown Mall,
Iju Road, Agege Lagos.
admin@opembooks.com
www.opembooks.com
08068448792, 08188315423

CONTENTS

DEDICATION

To my father –
Odunayo – for the game he loves.

Chapter 1

Kayode's school: a citadel of academics, sports and discipline

Kayode was a great lover of football. He had interest in the game in all forms: from talking about it to actual playing. He was indeed a football buff par excellence. He was about sixteen years of age and in his final year in a boarding college owned by a Christian missionary church in one of the urban areas of a state in the south-west of the country, Nigeria. The school, though in a purely traditional environment, could boast of student population like many in large, urban centers in the country. The co-educational status of the school made it the most populated school in the small town, and that boosted the social importance and influence of the school at that time.

Of all few schools that were in the small town and the neighboring towns, Kayode's school stood out as the most excellent in academics, sporting activities particularly in football competitions, in facilities, in staffing, and in hostel accommodation. In fact, in football the schools team stood out as the most endowed and most sophisticated team. While other teams appeared during any football match in apron-like jerseys, and played bare-foot or at most, in brown converse or rubber soccer boots, the school team had a beautiful set of jerseys and standard soccer shoes which made them an enviable team whenever they are on the field of play. In actual fact, their filing out on the football pitch was enough threat to any team. They were always in high spirit whenever they had to play any football match, because they were adequately motivated. They also did not have to come to football match venues in hired buses or by trekking like others, but in their newly-bought Peugeot J5 bus or any of their Toyota Coaster bus. Because of all these unequal things and the way they comported themselves around in other sporting events, other opposing teams always felt inferior; and more often than not, their losses always began at that very moment.

In Kayode's days in the school, he was the number one player. His records were unbeaten. He started featuring in the school feeder's team from his first year in the school, and by the second year, he had entered the main team. By his position as a top striker, he had to his credit over three dozen of goals in "professional" matches. He represented the school in football matches more than any other student by the time he got to his final year; automatically, he became the captain of the team; and by chance, he was liked by almost all the students. Besides, Kayode being very handsome attracted the attention of most girls in the school which created some level of envy among his male peers. Nevertheless, he was still well favoured by a large percentage of the entire school populace.

Kayode, because of his excellent performance, coupled with unspeakable ability he displayed at scoring goals, he was nicknamed "KAYOR-GOAL!" but the shortened form was KAYOR. This name was always on the lips of students whenever the school was playing a football match. As if the name was a charm for Kayode, whenever the shortened nickname was chanted hysterically, there would always be something positive that he would do to justify the shouting. Even though they did not all the time result in him scoring goal, yet his unrivalled performance was worth celebrating. It might be an exceptional display of skill or a most humbling dribbling pass an opponent. As far as football in Kayode's school and in surrounding towns was concerned, he was the "big boy".

Midway into Kayode's final year in the secondary school, precisely some weeks into the second term, preparation began for a crucial football match between Kayode's school and another school's team from another state. It was actually the final match of the President's Cup, a tournament that began in the penultimate year. The Federal Ministry of Sports had introduced the tournament in order to discover potentials and to reward talents. It was the first of the kind in history of the country. The competition was opened to all secondary schools across the country and it enjoyed the patronage and support of multinational companies because they considered that the president was keenly interested in it. The winning prize was too juicy that it further propelled the tempo of the competition among the participating schools. The prizes were such that the status of the winning school and the lives of players would never be the same again.

The stages of the tournament were so competitive that for any school to have made it to the final, the team must really be a good one and must have defeated other very good teams. The elimination stages began at the Local Government Level up to state level, and then to region before the two teams emerged to play the final. It was really a competitive tournament.

But heaven was on the side of Kayode's school as the team continued to progress through the stages till it gets to the final match. The profiles of the school and Kayode kept rising as the competition progressed. Many people did not believe that a school from hinterland could reach a final of the competition. The tournament was well received

Kayode on the football field

among the rank and file of schools as reflected in their massive participation. The only complaint that some schools had toward it was that it took a long time to get to the final. This made some schools to lose some of their best players who had graduated in the course of the tournament. It was only students of senior secondary schools that were eligible to be fielded. Schools that defaulted in this or any other regulations were penalized. The nation as a whole, particularly football enthusiasts that were interested in youth football, followed closely the competition. Big sport personalities were also involved. The more crucial matches were broadcast live, especially the final match which would be broadcast live as it promised to have in attendance the president himself with his counterpart from São Tomé and Príncipe as the special guest of honour. Some other important personalities were also expected. From the planning, it looked like it would be a great day.

Furthermore, it was planned that the President's trophy would be brought to the venue by a helicopter to add to the glamour and fun packaged for the closing ceremony. Everyone looked forward to the event. Expectations were very high in Kayode's school; preparations were in top gear for the match. The members of the school football team were to be camped in a hotel in Abuja, the Federal Capital Territory where the match would be played, two weeks ahead of the match.

Chapter 2

Preparation for the great Game

An inexplicable feverish condition enveloped Kayode's school the day they were to depart for Abuja. For the first time, they seemed to be generally caught with the feeling of inferiority and insecurity. The courageous ones among them feigned courage, but the ambience of fear and doubt was unexpectedly evident. That, notwithstanding, some students managed to instill confidence in the team by singing songs of encouragement before they left. The team and its supporters' club were conveyed in the school buses. The principal, Reverend Paulo, gave them a brief inspiring talk shortly before they took off for Abuja.

"Boys, there is nothing to worry about. You are going there to do us proud, for sure. I want you to know that we've put everything in place to make sure you enjoy the best so that you can perform optimally that day; be it financially, materially or even psychologically. I understand some of you want your mentors and parents there on that day. Someone like Kayode, I 've been reliably informed that your dad is a great source of inspiration to you. You don't worry; we will bring him along that day. Just be expecting some members of staff and myself to cheer you to victory on that day. Lastly, I want to warn the supporters' club members not to be a distraction to these boys. Let them concentrate. Is that okay? He appealed to all the students.

"Yes, sir" They all chorused

"That's good. Now, let me pray with you before you leave. The Holy book teaches us to commit whatever we want to do into the hands of God"

Everyone went silent.

"Our father which art in heaven..." He prayed and the boys made their way to the different buses while the principal had a final tête-à-tête with the games master who happened to be the one leading the contingents.

Before anyone knew what was happening, some female students had started shedding emotional tears. Kayode could not hold back his tears as they trickled down slowly on his face from where he sat by the window. He was not sure whether it was tears of joy or fear, but he was cocksure that a heavy burden was on him as far as that match is

Principal and Rev Paulo talking to the team

concerned. It was a make or mar match. All the years he had been winning without giving a thought for once as to how losing a match could look like. And for the first time, he wondered whether he would experience it in Abuja or not. He remembered the story of Mohammed Ali, as his father told him, when he lost a bout as a heavyweight boxing champion. According to his father, Mohammed Ali was left alone after the bout; no journalist hobnobbed with him as before, they all went after the winner. That day, according to him, afforded him the opportunity of knowing for the first time how losing a boxing bout could look like for a boxer.

"Is it my time to know?" He could not answer himself.

Chapter 3

The Dreamer

The day finally came and it was a unique day in Kayode's camp. News went round about some dreams a few of the boys had on the night preceding the D-day. As each day drew near, the atmosphere became increasingly tensed for the boys. That necessitated arduous training to which they subjected themselves, but there was a relief when the dream was relayed. Three boys who each had slept in different rooms had dreams all pointing to a winning match.

So, there was great joy in the camp. Everyone was invigorated. They jumped around in uncontrollable excitement and more or less did not train that morning.

How were the dreams relayed? Kayode happened to be one of the dreamers and his dream seemed to be the most comprehensive and detailed. He said, as he first confided in a trusted ally because he feared other strikers might be envious: "The game was tough but our performance was impressive. However, no goals came until the ninetieth minute. I saw our goalkeeper, Damola, gave a goal-kick and was headed by Kunle, and was then received by Pemi. Pemi passed it to the righthand side for me to continue." He continued.

"I took it and gave a long pass to the left side of the pitch, to divert opponent's attention from the right wing. As if on cue, I moved to the middle to get a pass from Loko. The ball was above me, but I jumped up to receive it on my chest. I brought it down to my feet. Within split of seconds, I could see there were only defenders and their goalkeeper before me. A little to the right, I swayed and then moved back to the left; they swayed a little. Then, I put the ball in between my legs and then tapped it to loop over me from behind pass the defenders. I moved with the ball with strong aim, for I knew the ball would go forward ahead of me going behind them. Before they could understand the whereabouts of the ball, I went past them, received it on my chest and brought it down again with speed. The goalkeeper made for my feet; I looped above him with a push for the ball to pass by him. I netted the ball into the net! I couldn't believe it. I scored the winning goal in the ninetieth minute. I did it. I made it. I guess I will carry the cup today or what do you think?" He asked.

Kayode in a dream lifting trophy

By the time Kayode finished narrating his dream, his friend's eyes were pulped open. He could not resist the joy. It was as if he just watched the match on television. Thanks to the descriptive story-telling ability of Kayode. He shouted for joy and it caught the attention of others. By the time he let the cat out of the bag, two other boys jumped up to corroborate it by telling their dreams which both had it that they won narrowly through a goal from Kayode. But whether narrowly or by a wide margin, the bottom line was that they won and that was enough joy for them. What thrilled them most was that the supernatural seemed to be giving them the opportunity of knowing the future. It was believed among them that dream was one of the ways men are able to see into the future.

"It shows God is in our camp" one of them said.

"Not just that, I think He graduated from our school!" Another said jokingly which provoked a hysterical laughter.

However, apart from the corporate joy in the camp; for Kayode personally, it looked more like the day of his own glory: his own day of success. All his fears were gone quickly and never had he been so optimistic in his entire life. He became so sure of the game that it reflected in the mood of everyone in the camp, even the officials; for he was their natural leader. Apart from the corporate victory

Kayode narrating his dream to his team

ahead, he saw it as crowning glory for his talent.
"This day, 11th September, I will score a most crucial and historic goal before the eyes of Mr. President and the whole world. I can see it!" He mused to himself. "There can't be any other strategic glory than this goal" He went on.
Thus, life came into the camp early that morning as a result of the sweet dreams from three boys, particularly that of the set boy, Kayor, which they all chose to accept as a forecast.
After the whole excitement, Kayode's friend, whom he trusted to have first told the dream, called him aside to make an observation.
"You know what I found?" He muttered
"Except you tell me." Kayode responded
"The power in using 'we' rather than 'I', my old uncle thought taught me, and I have since found it to be true."
"What's the meaning of that?" Perturbed, Kayode queried.
"Oh!" Painfully, he regretted. "You didn't get it." He bowed his head in sorrow leaving Kayode on the spot.
"What's the meaning of all this? You're leaving me?" Kayode retorted.
"You'll get it later." He said resignedly.

Chapter 4

Struggle for the great Trophy

At the match venue, the atmosphere was charged. Security operatives, both in uniform and mufti, were evenly distributed all over the place. This was expected, because in some minutes' time, the President would arrive in company of the São Tomé and Príncipe's counterpart. The members of his cabinet were already seated with other notable personalities from private concerns. The sound of helicopter could be heard from the open sky and students who formed the core of the people at the stadium were shouting, obviously awed by the mighty flying object. Their mouths were all shaking, apparently chewing gum graciously provided by a company co-sponsoring the event.

There was a mixture of joy and tension in the air. Everywhere in the stadium was agog with excitement. Soon, the programme started with the voice of the compere heard over the loudspeaker calling for attention of everyone. He took time to introduce the guests and to intimate the audience with the lined-up programme of activities for the day. He also introduced and brought to a special row of seats not far from the VIP seat, the third-place match winners. With that under way, the President arrived and every movement of persons literally ceased.

Who will not expect such? Everything was put on hold until the President and his colleagues from São Tomé and Príncipe took their seat. Almost immediately, the national Anthem was rendered and that further got the atmosphere charged as the rendition was electrifying. Indeed, the students' psychological feeling was gratified and it showed on their faces. It was amazing to observe the effect of the National Anthem being sung by those kids in the presence of their Number One Citizen. They felt great, and they learned a sense of belonging, too.

One item followed another as the President mounted the podium to give a very short speech on his government's objective for organizing the tournament and the hope of its continuity. As expected, people expressed skepticism on its continuity. But that was just by the way. The major concern of most people at the venue was the final football match which was about to kick off. It was as if the ninety minutes' game should be compressed into thirty minutes for them to quickly know the winner.

In the dressing room, Kayode appears unperturbed. Being the captain, he was the first boy on the lane as they awaited the announcement to file out. His father was also present as well as Reverend Paulo, the principal. The two of them became much like twins since they arrived early that morning. They had never ceased to give the boys various motivational tip to perform excellently in the match.

In one of the moments Kayode had with his father, he told his father about the dream he had the previous night and his excitement.

"That's good..." His father had said; "but, put your mind off that. This may not be the game."

"This is the game, daddy" He stated confidently. "I 've seen two other things I saw in the dream take place since we arrived at the stadium"

"Is that so?" His father inquired

"Yes, Dad. This is the day the Lord has made"

"Well...well," His father agreed reluctantly; "but, don't forget that you are now in the reality. Dreams don't live themselves out, you've got to do. Just be focused and play your game as expected. Remember as I always tell you, though you are a striker, the game is not all about you alone. Don't be unnecessarily ambitious or selfish with the ball."

Kayode's father advising him in dressing room

As Kayode nodded, his father quipped in. “Lest I forget, don't be intimidated by the presence of big people in the stadium and don't try to impress. Just be your authentic self! Be calm and cool, alright?”

“I will, Dad.” He snapped

Meanwhile, as they waited the announcement, the boys from the other team took some time to observe them, perhaps to see if they could feel their pulse but because of the competitive nature of the match and their immaturity, they refused to mix or greet one another.

As the match anchor announced the name of the other team to file out, Kayode's father grabbed his son's hands forcefully and with an expression of affinity for his boy, he said, “I've always known you will do us proud one day.” He paused as both eyes met fixedly. “I don't mind if today is one of the days” His father concluded slowly.

“I remain your boy, Dad; and I have a feeling that the day has come”

“I am not in a hurry anyway.”

“So am I; but I'm hungry for it.” His voice was determined and full of courage.

“You have my prayers.”

“Thank you, Dad.”

Kayode and his father were lost in the moment. It took the boy behind Kayode to bring his consciousness back into the room

“It's our turn, Kayor.” The boy announced.

“See you at the end of the match, son.” His father said and left his hands. As they filed out bouncing in their kits, his father closed his eyes in a meditative prayer.

Chapter 5

The Game that never was

The President and his counterpart came down to shake hands with the boys as they filed out on the pitch. The President attended to the other team first before coming to Kayode's team. As the captain of his team, Kayode was the one, with the assistance of the match officials, introducing each of the players to the Presidents.

However, Kayode's introduction was interrupted mid-way by one of the match officials.

"This is Kayode Akinnusi. Mr. President. He is the boy having a tie with Kazeem Bello as the highest goal scorer so far." The official added.

"Hmm! So, you are the KAYOR-GOAL? I have been hearing about that name since the competition started." The President exclaimed evincing the excitement of a little child who had just seen his hero.

One of the match officials introducing kayode to the The President

Kayode felt abashed though he savoured the moment of such record before the President moved to the next team member. It was at that point it dawned on him that he was the highest goal scorer alongside a striker in the opposing team. All that occupied his mind thereafter was, "if only I can increase the tally today." He soon jolted back as the cool hands of Mr. President touched his. He cherished it and felt great having that quick moment with the President. Soon, the President was returning to his seat and the referee took the captains of the two teams through the normal rituals on the field of play before the game starts. The noise going on at the stadium by the spectators and the supporters' club on both sides was deafening. Drumbeats suddenly went louder than before. Trumpets and tambourine were not left out in the noise making. Each of the team supporters' club seemed desperate to cheer its team to victory. Some of them carried placards with various inscriptions:

"THE FINAL SHOWDOWN."

"THE DAY OF SEPARATIONS."

"GO FOR GOALS KAYORGOAL!"

"THE KING OF GOALS."

Some of them appeared rather offensive or what will one

say of one like this:
'THE BUSH BOY MUST FALL FLAT". This was targeted to Kayode's school. There was another with this inscription evidencing confidence
"OUR DEFENCE IS AS STRONG AS OLUMO ROCK". They drew a reference to a mountain that was believed to offer refuge for the Egba people during the wars hundreds of years ago.
Members of each side soon gathered round themselves for prayers. In Kayode's side, it was the goalkeeper who led the prayers.
"Dear Father in heaven, as we saw in our dream, please do so unto us in the name of your Holy Child, Jesus Christ."
He said the simple prayer and all of them disperse to their respective wings, not without a final passing remark of encouragement or caution from one another. While others made short dashes on the pitch, the mood was so sobering for Kayode to do that. He seemed to be communicating within himself.
"Now is the time for the son of man." He muttered slowly with a little swing of his arms as he made for the center of the field. Not quite long, the stage was set for the kick off. Kayode's leg was on the ball as he paced up and down meditatively.

"The hour has come." He said finally to himself before the referee blew the whistle to start the match. At exactly four o'clock, the match started with a pass from Kayode to a team mate.

"The dream had just begun." Kayode seemed to have said. Kayode's father, where he sat, he really hoped the day would be his son's day of glory. He sensed the quest of personal glory in his son more than ever before. He perceived it may have been so because of the large retinue of important personalities in the stadium including those there to hunt for talents. He had cautioned him to remain his authentic self and not to try to impress unnecessarily. Despite the warning, he could see that in his son's mode of play, as the match progressed. Nevertheless, he followed every move of the ball with prayer in his heart for his son's team. He was not the only one apprehensive of the match. Everyone on the bench was apprehensive too. Anytime the ball moved in the direction of their opponent, those that were over-anxious would jump out of their seat; while those had a bit of control on their pulses would sit on the edge of their seat. If the ball moved them against in such a dimension that they couldn't contain, they would shout and gesture as if they are on the field of play to see if perhaps, they could do a rescue work for their team.

The two teams were really having a great game. Kayode had some spectacular moves, and the opposing goalkeeper did really help his team with some brilliant saves. It was obvious that Kayode capitalized on the lapses of the defenders a few times. For the most part, he had at least two defenders to tackle him. It was a herculean task beating them, but it also served as encouragement for him; because he never forgot that in the dream, he took the ball past two defenders. Anytime the ball got to him, he would find himself thinking along that line while the play was on. "Now is the time" but it never happened. That did not, however, dampen his belief in his dream of scoring the winning goal. He believed very strongly that the goal would still come.

The first forty-five minutes of the game ended goal-less. In the dressing room, comments of the people around them showed the two had a tough first half, but Kayode's team's performance was adjudged the better. With that, Kayode was optimistic. The words of a former American President came to his mind. The American president had expressed in his autobiography that he thanked God for allowing him to his dream. He pondered over it while he rested and quietly prayed that he would be able to say that too, at the end of the match. He had come to know much about these

Kayode dribbling past two defenders

important personalities through his father's library, for they were stuffed with biographies and autobiographies. Those that were too voluminous were fearful for him to pick; but by the time his father told him a little of the story, he would find the motivation to pick it up and read. It was from this library that he fell in love with Pele of Brazil through his book, *My Life and the Beautiful Game*. He had found himself greatly motivated and inspired through these books.

However, in the middle of encomiums being showered on the team, a renowned footballer who apparently favoured their team to win, came down on them with a stern warning. They were glad to see him anyway and that perhaps watered down the gravity of his warning. Not very many of them paid attention to what he said. They were too awe struck.

He began, "If you guys are willing to sacrifice some personal glory particularly on the front end, your team should win"

The second half started obviously with greater determination in Kayode. He knew this was just the moment he has been waiting for. He was all over the pitch just desperately in search of the ball, and whenever he got it, he would display excellently. Most of the spectators could see his rugged determination to get a goal. He got so close to some goals but never got the ball at the back of the net. His efforts met with praises and the appreciation spurred him to put in more. In the second hand, he did less of dribbling and tried a bit more shots at the goal than distributing the ball. Whenever he had a free moment on the pitch, he would hear his name being chanted like never before and he would feel a great burden to deliver a goal for his school. He knew how his fans would feel at such a moment having been an ardent fan of the Super Eagles of Nigeria whenever they are on the field of play.

"All eyes are on you." He heard something telling him.

He felt terribly bad and frustrated that, despite his frantic efforts, the goal had refused to come. There was no watch on him but he knew that time was fast running out. The faces of spectators suggest expectations including the President and others in the VIP section, and though they seemed to favour Kayode's school based on their spectacular performance thus far, there was nothing anyone could do about it. To say the least, by the timing, the spectators knew that whichever of the teams that score would carry the day. The tension was at its peak for the two teams and spectators.

Not long afterwards, barely ten minutes to the end of the

match, the goalkeeper of Kayode's team, out of his anxiety to contribute to working out a goal went a little past his box to launch the ball into the opponent's side. A fellow team mate controlled the ball and gave it to Kayode. Quickly, he switched it in a long pass from the right wing to the left. In a jiffy, the boy sent it into the midst of payers at the mouth of box 18 for a contest. Somehow, Kayode made away with the ball from among them. It was greeted with a loud applause. All eyes followed his next moved with all curiosity to see if this this goal they have all been waiting to see in the match, for so it seemed. He dribbled past the first and the next defender and attempted dribbling the goalkeeper, too whilst ignoring a fellow team mate at a more advantageous position to receive and score the ball. At that attempt alone, the whole team went agog in excitement. Some would have him pass the ball to the team mate while some would have him finish what he started but nobody could decide for him at that moment. Be that as it may, it was just the super exciting moment they had all been waiting for. The whole spectators in the stadium literally stood up to their feet chanting,

"KAYORGOAL! KAYORGOAL! KAYORGOAL!"

The goalkeeper, however, foiled the attempt brilliantly, to everyone's utter amazement by going for the ball right on

Kayode's feet before he succeeds in dribbling past him. Kayode loped into the air but not without stamping his soccer boot, out of disappointment, on the head of the goalkeeper. With no struggle, the goalkeeper who was already holding the ball let go of it, grabbing his head and writhing in pain. Blood was oozing out of his head. That kept the match on hold for a while. Furthermore, the referee adjudged Kayode's moves as intentional foul, and without wasting time, he reached for his red card. Kayode was sent out of the match! He could not believe he saw a red card but it was. He stood there frozen for seconds.

“Is that a red card?” His eyes evinced shock as he inquired from a team mate. He did not get answer. The team mate was also shocked to confirm it. He had to confirm it again by himself. It was a rude shock. It meant the end of, not just the match, but the dream. It shook him to the bone marrow.

Like a baby, Kayode bawled out crying dejectedly that day. As he was being ushered out of the pitch, he still thought it was a dream that he should be awaken out of, but it was not to be. His dream was not to be anymore. That left his team disoriented, and their end was worse.

Swiftly, in an opportunistic adventure of their disoriented spirit, the opposing team took chances and less than five minutes after Kayode's exit, they scored a goal. Kayode

The referee issuing Kayode a red card

was the more moved to tears. It was simply uncontrollable. He regretted the scenario, and really felt he could become so powerful to reverse the turn of events, but alas, he has no such powers and that further engendered his anger with himself. It was not the day he had wished for. He felt guilty that he did what he did which was very unusual for him in his football years so far. He wept so much that even his father and the golden boot he won alongside Kazeem could not placate him. As his joy was great in the morning, so was his harrowing sorrow by the evening of that day. What a disaster!

He felt really bad about himself and thought he would never be able to forget the day that his bad temperament had cost him a glorious moment but his father encouraged him. It was not the game he had in mind.

Glossary of words and their meanings as used in the story.

(be) focused:	attending to what one wants to do specifically
(be) intimidated:	frightened or threatened somebody into doing something
abashed:	(felt) embarrassed and ashamed
academics:	subjects involving a lot of reading and studying
adjudged:	made an opinion about somebody based on some facts
agog:	excited
alarming:	surprising
ally:	a friend or a team member
ambience:	atmosphere
apprehensive:	nervous that some unpleasant things may occur
ardent:	very enthusiastic
arduous:	difficult to achieve
autobiography:	life stories of a person written by the person
bare-footed:	not wearing anything on one's feet
bawled:	cried out loudly
beamed:	smiled radiantly
biographies:	life stories of someone written by another person
bottom-line:	the main point

bout:	a turn or round
buff:	a person who knows a lot about a game
capitalizing:	turning into one's advantage
charm:	the quality of arousing admiration
cocksure:	very sure; definite
comport:	to behave oneself
compere:	a master of ceremony
comprehensive:	containing full details
compressed:	pressed together
confided:	to tell someone about a secret
contingent:	a team
core hinterland:	rural area
corroborate:	to provide supporting facts supporting a statement
dampen:	to discourage
defaulted:	failed
desperately:	very seriously
disoriented:	lacking interest and confused
distraction:	something that takes away one's attention
electrifying:	exciting, captivating
emotional:	showing strong feelings
encomiums:	high praises
encounter:	to meet face to face, especially unexpectedly
engendered:	encouraged to make something happen
enveloped:	covered entirely
enviable:	desirable

envious:	feeling jealous
exceptional:	unusual
excitement:	state of being happy
exclaimed:	said loudly and suddenly
featuring:	taking part in
feeder (team):	reserved team from where replacements are drawn or supplied
feign:	to pretend feverish (condition) anxious moment
filing-out:	walking in a line one after the other in a particular direction
flock around:	to gather in crowd around someone
foiled:	stopped or prevent something from happening
football pitch:	ground prepared for playing football
forecast:	to predict things before happening
frantic:	furious
frustrated:	disappointed
gesture:	speaking by moving part of one's body
glamour:	attraction
goal-less:	neither team scoring a goal
gratified:	pleasing
harrowing:	very shocking and upsetting
herculean:	extremely difficult
hobnobbed:	talk informally with
hold back:	to keep away from
hysterical:	extremely funny
immaturity:	a state of not being fully developed

inexplicable:	difficult to explain
inspiration:	encouragement
(to) intimate:	to hint someone of an idea
invigorating:	strengthened
jersey:	smart wear with no buttons worn by footballers
jiffy:	in an instant
jolted:	shake suddenly
juicy:	generous and attractive
lapses:	failures
let the cat out of the bag:	speak out the secret
looped above:	jumped above
loped:	leapt, ran with a long stride
made for:	tried to seize
make or mar:	to be the crucial test that brings success or failure
marrow:	a soft substance that fills the hollow part of the bone
meditatively:	consider deeply
mentor:	counseller; adviser
missionaries:	persons sent to a foreign country to teach about the Christian faith
motivated to:	induced to
multinational:	a large business company which operates in many countries

mused:	meditated
muttered:	said something very quietly
neighbouring:	situated near
netted (the ball):	kicked (the ball) to score a goal
nicknamed:	gave a name to someone in sporting familiarity
oozing:	coming out of
opponent:	one who opposes
opportunistic:	taking advantage of a situation
optimally:	most favourably
optimistic:	most hopeful
outings:	occasions when competitors take part in a competition
paced:	walked slowly and meaningfully
par excellence:	superior to all others of the same type
penultimate:	last but one
perturbed:	disturbed greatly
placate:	(to) make someone less angry
podium:	a raised platform for standing on to address people
pondered:	thought over
potentials:	possibilities
psychological:	having to do with a persons mind and how it works
pulped open:	made eyes wide open for a purpose

cue:	the part or a role one has to play
quipped in:	cut in sharply as in a conversation
records:	achievements
reluctantly:	grudgingly
renowned:	famous
resist:	(to) oppose
retinue:	a body or group of people
retorted:	remarked
reverse (to):	change a previous decision
rituals:	repeated series of actions of doing the something with the same object
rugged:	rough
savour:	taste, flavour
skepticism:	an attitude of doubting
snapped:	spoke impatiently and angrily
sobering:	making someone playing sober
sophisticated:	very refined and modern
spectacular:	very impressive
spurred:	urged on
staffing:	people who working in a school
status:	rank, importance, e.g of a school among others
strategic:	meant or done to achieve a particular purpose
swayed:	moved slowly from one side to side

switched:	turned to another point
tapped:	touched a part of the body slightly
temperament:	having tendency to become angry or easily upset
tense:	tight; charged
tensed up:	became very nervous and worrisome
tête-à-tête:	private conversation between two persons
the envy of:	the pride of
threat:	possibility of being a danger or fear to others
tips:	hints
top gear:	high spirit (of doing things)
top striker:	prolific goal scorer
tournament:	a series of games to determine winning team
traditional:	following old methods
unbeaten:	never defeated; undefeated
uncontrollable:	that cannot be control
unique:	distinctly unequalled; very special
unperturbed:	undisturbed or not anxious
ushered:	showed someone (out of a place)
vintage:	of good quality
whereabouts:	movements around

ANOTHER BOOK BY THE AUTHOR

The Difference We Can Make

Plays for Schools

The Difference We Can Make captures the struggles a woman commissioner faces for daring to be different.

Will She Marry Me? is a comical foray into the love affair of a police officer whose fiancée is in a conflict with his choice of job.

www.ingramcontent.com/pod-product-compliance
Lightning Source LLC
LaVergne TN
LVHW041256150826
845673LV00008B/2616

* 9 7 8 9 7 8 7 8 5 9 9 9 5 *